For Sam, forever young

C.F.

PUFFIN BOOKS

Published by the Penguin Group

Penguin Books Ltd, 80 Strand, London WC2R 0RL, England

Penguin Group (USA) Inc., 375 Hudson Street, New York, New York 10014, USA

Penguin Group (Canada), 10 Alcorn Avenue, Toronto, Ontario, Canada M4V 3B2 (a division of Pearson Penguin Canada Inc.)

Penguin Ireland, 25 St Stephen's Green, Dublin 2, Ireland (a division of Penguin Books Ltd)

Penguin Group (Australia), 250 Camberwell Road, Camberwell, Victoria 3124, Australia (a division of Pearson Australia Group Pty Ltd)

Penguin Books India Pvt Ltd, 11 Community Centre, Panchsheel Park, New Delhi – 110 017, India

Penguin Group (NZ), cnr Airborne and Rosedale Roads, Albany, Auckland 1310, New Zealand (a division of Pearson New Zealand Ltd)

Penguin Books (South Africa) (Pty) Ltd, 24 Sturdee Avenue, Rosebank, Johannesburg 2196, South Africa

Penguin Books Ltd, Registered Offices: 80 Strand, London WC2R 0RL, England

www.penguin.com

Published 2005

3 5 7 9 10 8 6 4

Text copyright © Sam McBratney, 2005
Illustrations copyright © Charles Fuge, 2005

The moral right of the author and illustrator has been asserted

Set in Aunt Mildred
Made and printed in China

British Library Cataloguing in Publication Data
A CIP catalogue record for this book is available from the British Library

ISBN 0-141-38081-0

It's Lovely When You Smile

Sam McBratney
Charles Fuge

PUFFIN

It was a lovely summer morning,
but Roo was feeling grumpy
and he didn't know why.

He was feeling so grumpy that
he didn't even want to play.

"What's wrong with you this morning?"
asked his mother.
"Nothing," said Roo.
"You should smile," his mother said.
"Everybody feels better
when they smile."

But Little Roo wasn't in a smiling mood today,
not even when his mother tickled him gently.
"Did I see a tiny smile?" she asked.
"Just one?"

"No!" said Roo.
"You didn't."

It was the
kind of game that
little kangaroos love to play!

His mum reached out and flipped him up head over heels.

But would it work this grumpy morning?

No. Little Roo did **not** smile.

Not even a teeny-weeny one.

His mother **skipped** into a hollow

tree where they liked to **play**.

She popped her head through

a hole in the trunk.

"**Smile!**"

"I still don't want to," said Little Roo.

"Oh dear," said his mum. So she gathered up some dry leaves, tossed them into the air and all the leaves came down on Little Roo.

He looked **so** funny!
"I think I can see a **smile** this time,"
laughed his mum.
"Just a bit of
a one . . . ?"

"You don't," said Roo. "I'm NOT smiling."
"Oh well," sighed his mother.

It was time for breakfast.
Little Roo's mum lifted him up. "Let's go down
the hill together and find something to eat."
"I'm **not** hungry," said Roo grumpily.
"But I'm hungry," said his mum.
"Come on."

"Hold on tight!"

And off they went.

Halfway down the hill there was a hole.

It wasn't a deep hole, but it was a wide hole,

and a **muddy-at-the-bottom** hole.

"Look out!" cried Roo.

But his mum was doing silly hops

from side to side instead

of looking

where

she

was

going

AND . . .

...slippity

...slippity

...slide

and...

... slop!
Right into
the hole.

Roo himself was muddy all over.
Then he looked at his mother, who was soaking wet and
slimy from the tops of her ears to the tips of her toes.

And Little Roo couldn't do anything else.

He just
had
to . . .

...smile!

"It's lovely when you smile."